# Memoirs of a TORTOISE

By Devin Scillian and Illustrated by Tim Bowers

## SLEEPING BEAR PRESS™

2395 South Huron Parkway, Suite 200
Ann Arbor, MI 48104
www.sleepingbearpress.com

Printed and bound in the United States.

10 9 8 7 6 5 4 3 2

Library of Congress Cataloging-in-Publication Data

Names: Scillian, Devin, author. | Bowers, Tim, illustrator.
Title: Memoirs of a tortoise / by Devin Scillian ; illustrated by Tim Bowers.
Description: Ann Arbor, Michigan : Sleeping Bear Press, [2020] | Audience:
Ages 4-8. | Summary: Oliver the tortoise looks back on his happy life as
he wonders why his pet human, Ike, who he has had for eighty years, has
stopped visiting the garden.
Identifiers: LCCN 2019047133 | ISBN 9781534110199 (hardcover)
Subjects: CYAC: Turtles—Fiction. | Pets—Fiction. | Death—Fiction.
Classification: LCC PZ7.S41269 Mft 2020 | DDC [E]—dc23
LC record available at https://lccn.loc.gov/2019047133

In loving memory of Isaac Hendershot and Theodore Mueller.

—Devin

To Grady, Caleb, and Brylie.

—Tim

## April

It's spring.

The garden is sunny and warm. I think April is my favorite month of the year.

It's a glorious day and Ike just brought me a plate of lettuce and dandelions and a bright, crunchy apple.

Ike is my pet. I love Ike. And Ike loves me. He runs his hand across my shell and tells me so.

This, this is life and it's beautiful.

## May

It rained last night. The whole garden is fresh and new. I can smell the gardenias and the lilacs. Eighty times I've watched spring arrive in the garden, and it's always perfect.

Ike throws a stick and says, "Oliver, fetch!" But we just laugh because we both know I'm not chasing a silly stick. We do this every day.

I think there's a hibiscus blooming on the other side of the garden. I'll go look.

## June

Wow, what a trip. All the way across the garden and now I'm sitting in a forest of hibiscus.

I like to take my time in the garden. Ike is like me. He takes his time.

My mother always says, "The whole world is in a hurry. They miss so much."

I'm not missing anything, including the honeydew melon Ike gave me this morning. Don't tell Ike, but I would definitely fetch honeydew melon.

## July

Ike is sitting under his favorite sycamore tree, reading a book. I'm next to him and this is my favorite time of all, just me and Ike and this beautiful garden. How long can we sit here? How about forever?

Forever would be
fine with me.

## August

It's hot today. Ike fills the baby pool and splashes me with water. Now I'm soaking wet and I try to pretend I'm angry, but Ike just laughs, and that makes me laugh and so we laugh together.

A banana for dinner.

Night takes over and Ike looks up at all of the stars in the sky and whistles.

# September

Life slows down this time of year. The days are getting shorter. There's a coolness in the breeze. Even Ike is slower. He's taking lots of naps in the garden. That's okay with me. I watch a leaf fall from the sycamore and I decide I'm going to surprise Ike. The next time he throws the stick, I'm going to fetch it. He won't believe it.

## October

Fall is here. It's time to put the baby pool and the garden hose away, but no one does. I haven't seen Ike for a few days. He hasn't brought me anything to eat. It's okay. I can eat some of the pumpkin in the garden. But where is Ike?

## November

I'm afraid Ike is gone.

People have come to visit, and they're very sad. And that makes me sad.

Ike was still so young. He was 80 years old. Just like me. We were practically twins! I thought we were going to grow old together.

Ike, where have you gone?

## December

My mother is 137 years old. Sometimes I think she knows everything. It's a long way to her garden. But I think she's the only one I can talk to. If anyone knows why Ike left me, it will be Mother.

## January

There are ten gardens between my mother and me. I used to tell my mother that I wished I could fly and she would say, "You can have a shell or you can have wings, but you can't have both."

I don't know.

I think some beetles have both. But I don't
want to be a beetle, so I keep walking.

## February

Today I'm in Mother's garden. Mother is sitting in the one sunbeam that cuts through the clouds. She has a lot of wrinkles and her shell is worn and smooth. When she sees me, she smiles wide and her eyes sparkle.

"Mother, I'm so sad. Ike is gone."

"Oh, Oliver," she says. "Ike loved you so very much."

"But, Mother," I say, "why do we have to lose people?
Why couldn't Ike stay with me?"

Mother smiles. She closes her eyes and raises her head to the sun.

"We only get to have pets in our lives for a little while," she says.
"They don't live as long as we do. So we have to enjoy them every
day. And when they're gone, we count all those beautiful days we
were lucky enough to have them with us. We're so lucky."

## March

I am on my way back to my garden. Every step I take I think about what Mother said. I know she's right. She's always right. But I don't think my garden will ever be the same.

## April

I'm back home. Yes, back home, and it feels like where I belong.

For the 81st time, spring has come to my garden. As I look at
the sycamore tree, I hear the door and without thinking,
I turn to look for Ike. But Ike isn't there.

It's Ted.

Ted is Ike's son.

He is bringing me a tray of lettuce and dandelions and a bright, crunchy apple. He runs his hand along my shell and says, "I'm so glad you came home, Oliver. It's you and me now."

He picks up a stick and asks, "You want to play fetch?"

And for the first time in a long time, I laugh.

I think April is my favorite month of the year.

And this, for me and Ted, this is life.

Mother was right.

I'm so lucky.